Doodle Dog

Eric Seltzer

ALADDIN
New York London Toronto Sydney

For Mom,
the real poet, with love

ALADDIN PAPERBACKS
An imprint of Simon & Schuster Children's Publishing Division
1230 Avenue of the Americas, New York, NY 10020
Copyright © 2005 by Eric Seltzer
All rights reserved, including the right of
reproduction in whole or in part in any form.
READY-TO-READ, ALADDIN PAPERBACKS, and colophon are
registered trademarks of Simon & Schuster, Inc.
Designed by Lisa Vega
The text of this book was set in CenturyOldst BT.
Printed in the United States of America
First Aladdin Paperbacks edition August 2005
2 4 6 8 10 9 7 5 3 1
Library of Congress Cataloging-in-Publication Data
Seltzer, Eric.
Doodle Dog / by Eric Seltzer.
p. cm.
Summary: Doodle Dog, a talented artist, comes to the
rescue of his less artistic friends.
ISBN 0-689-85910-4 (Aladdin pbk.)—ISBN 0-689-85913-9 (library)
[1. Art—Fiction. 2. Dogs—Fiction. 3. Animals—Fiction.
4. Stories in rhyme.] I. Title.
PZ8.3.S4665Do 2005
[E]—dc21 2003009527

Monday morning.
Rise and shine.

Scratch at six.

Sniff at nine.

My pal King
gives me a call.

"Bring pad and pens.
Bring paint and all."

Time for art.

My tail wags.

Rushing, I forget
some bags.

"First," says King,
"Pig made a card."

Drawing hearts
was way too hard!

I grab a pad
and show her how.

Pig says, "Thanks!
I love it now!"

King and I
say our good-byes.

Red
Dye

Yellow
Dye

Blue
Dye

Racing, I forget
my dyes.

Bear is next.

He had a scare.

"Help!" he says.

"Blue everywhere!"

I take a brush
from my art kit.

Now Bear loves
to sip and sit.

17.

No paint with Pig.

No dyes with Bear.

We even check
with Madam Hare.

There was nothing
at the fair.

There was nothing
by the sea.

There was nothing
in the park.

There was nothing
up the tree.

After snooping
through the Ritz,
we decide
to call it quits.

Back at home
a big surprise—
inside are . . .

MY ART SUPPLIES!

Paste and pencils,

brushes, strings.

In one box
were all my things!

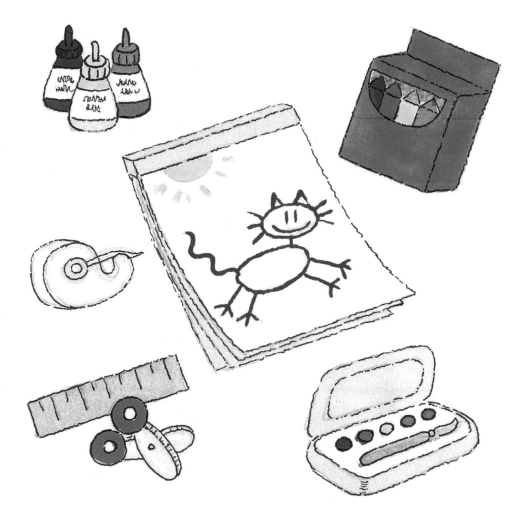

I see a note
from Pig and Bear.

"Bear found your stuff
under his chair."

Monday night,
I go to bed.
Pals and art
dance in my head.

Follow Doodle to the stars!